Little Star

adapted by Sarah Willson
based on the teleplay by Eric Weiner
illustrated by the Thompson Bros.

SIMON AND SCHUSTER

Based on the TV series DORA THE EXPLORER as seen on Nick Jr.

SIMON AND SCHUSTER
First published in Great Britain in 2006 by Simon & Schuster UK Ltd
1st Floor, 222 Gray's Inn Road, London WC1X 8HB

Originally published in the USA in 2002 by Simon Spotlight,
an imprint of Simon & Schuster Children's Division, New York.

A CIP catalogue record for this book is available from the British Library

ISBN 978-0-85707-432-4

Printed in China
10 9 8 7 6 5 4 3

Visit our websites: www.simonandschuster.co.uk
www.nick.co.uk

¡Hola! I'm Dora and this is my friend Boots. Do you like to make wishes? Every night before I go to bed I make a wish on the first star I see in the sky. There's Little Star! Can you see her up there next to her friend the Moon?

Oh, no! A comet has just knocked Little Star out of the sky and she's falling to the ground.

We have to get Little Star back home to the Moon, so that everyone can make their wishes. Will you help us?

How can we get Little Star up to the moon? Let's ask the map. Say, "Map!"

Map says we have to cross the Troll Bridge, then go past Tico's Tree, and that's how we'll get to Tall Mountain. If we climb Tall Mountain, we can take Little Star home to the Moon.

We made it to the Troll Bridge, but the Grumpy Old Troll won't let us cross over his bridge unless we solve his riddle. Will you help us solve it?

The Grumpy Old Troll says, "Star light, star bright. Can you see the stars so bright? Star light, star bright, how many stars are there tonight?"

Can you count the stars? Don't forget to count Little Star!

Eleven stars! You solved the riddle! Thanks for helping.
Now we can cross the bridge. Next is Tico's Tree.
Can you see it?

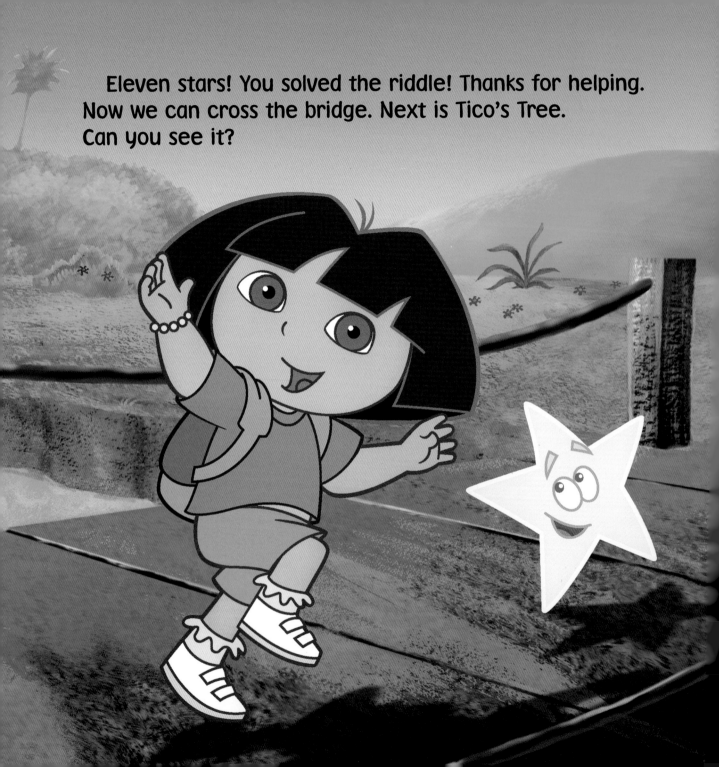

¡Vámonos! Let's get Little Star home to the Moon, so everyone can make their wishes!

This is our friend Tico the squirrel's house. *¡Hola,* Tico! Uh-oh. I hear Swiper the fox! I think that sneaky fox is trying to swipe Little Star. If you see Swiper, say, "Swiper, no swiping!"

You did it! You saved Little Star. Now we have to go to Tall Mountain. Do you see Tall Mountain?

There it is right underneath the Moon. Come on, we have to hurry! It's getting late!

We made it to the top of Tall Mountain! Little Star is almost home. But how are we going to get Little Star back up to the Moon? Let's stop and think.

I know! We can throw her back up to the moon! Can you help us?

Okay, cup your hands together. Now, on the count of three, I need you to throw your hands up in the air.

One . . . two . . . three. There she goes!

Good throw! We did it. Little Star made it all the way
home to her friend the Moon! Thanks for your help!

Now we can make our wishes.

Star light, star bright,
first star I see tonight.
I wish I may, I wish I might,
have this wish I wish tonight.

I wish that I could see Little Star every night.

Now you make your wish.

I hope it comes true! Good night!